2/16/10

SURFING

By S.L. Hamilton

Published by ABDO Publishing Company, 8000 West 78th Street, Suite 310, Edina, MN 55439. Copyright ©2010 by Abdo Consulting Group, Inc. International copyrights reserved in all countries. No part of this book may be reproduced in any form without written permission from the publisher. A&D Xtreme™ is a trademark and logo of ABDO Publishing Company.

Printed in the United States of America, North Mankato, Minnesota.
102009
012010

 PRINTED ON RECYCLED PAPER

Editor: John Hamilton
Graphic Design: Sue Hamilton
Cover Design: John Hamilton
Cover Photo: Getty Images
Interior Photos: Adam Weathered-pgs 1, 2, 3, 12, 13 & 26; AP-pgs 10, 11 & 29; Bishop Museum-pg 6; Corbis-pgs 17 & 27; Getty Images-pgs 5, 7, 8, 9, 14, 15, 20, 21, 22, 23, 24, 25, 26, 27, 28 & 32; iStockphoto-pgs 19, 30 & 31; National Geographic-pgs 18 & 19; Photo Researchers-pg 22.

Library of Congress Cataloging-in-Publication Data

Hamilton, Sue L., 1959-
  Surfing / S.L. Hamilton.
    p. cm. -- (Xtreme sports)
  Includes index.
  ISBN 978-1-61613-005-3
  1. Surfing--Juvenile literature. I. Title.
  GV839.55.H36 2010
  797.3'2--dc22
                            2009039942

CONTENTS

Surfing is defined as riding the crest of a wave on a surfboard. In reality, the sport pits a human being against the most powerful forces of nature: water and wind.

Xtreme Quote

"If you're out there with nothing but your body, your wits, and your surfboard, that can be your coffin." ~Bruce Jenkins

SURFING

Today's stand-up surfing began in Polynesia and Hawaii hundreds of years ago. Although commoners and chiefs both enjoyed surfing, it was known as the "sport of kings." Chiefs rode standing up (as opposed to being on their knees or bellies) on hardwood boards as long as 24 feet (7 m).

KINGS

"...this man felt the most supreme pleasure while he was driven on so fast and smoothly by the sea." ~Captain Cook, 1777

SURF

The sport of surfing really became popular in the 1960s. It has continued to grow and change. Today, surfers use a variety of surfboards to catch and ride the waves.

BOARDS

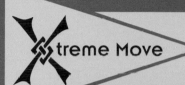

Xtreme Move To hang five, a surfer walks up the board until the toes of one foot hang over the tip.

Long-boarding

People who go "longboarding" use a surfboard that is more than 9 feet (3 m) in length. The length and heaviness of a longboard makes it easier to paddle and to catch a wave. A longboard surfer can ride even very small waves.

Xtreme Quote

"The glide is effortless... it's like driving a Rolls instead of a Porsche." ~Kevin Kinnear on longboards

Xtreme Fact Shortboards are designed to provide advanced surfers with power, speed, & control.

Shortboards became
popular in the late
1960s. At less than
7 feet (2 m) in length,
and weighing about
10 pounds (5 kg), the
light, maneuverable
boards began to
take over the sport.
However, shortboards
are difficult to paddle
and control. But
for tight turns
and cutbacks into
the waves, many
advanced surfers
prefer shortboards.

BIG-WAVE

> **Xtreme Quote** "A big wave has the destructive capacity of a major landslide or avalanche." ~The Complete Guide to Surfing

RIDING

Big-wave surfing pits a surfer against giant 16- to 50-foot (5-15 m) waves. To paddle fast enough to catch these killer waves, surfers use longer, heavier, and more streamlined surfboards known as "guns."

Tow-In Surfing

To catch big waves, a surfer must paddle quickly and intensely to overcome the trough-to-crest flow of water. A modern solution is for the surfer to be towed behind a boat or jet ski and thrust into the wave. After the waterski-style launch, the surfer drops the tow rope, and the rider is on his or her own with the monstrous wave.

Xtreme Quote

"The only way you can really prepare for big waves is to ride big waves... Maybe we'll die trying, but we'll go out and give it a shot." ~Mark Foo, died surfing 1994

Kiteboarders are strapped onto boards, while hand-controlled kites are harnessed to their waists. The wind-driven kites speed riders across the water or lift them up in the air for aerial tricks. While kiteboarders love the excitement, it is also dangerous. Riders risk being slammed into objects or trapped underwater by their kites.

Sails, Paddles, and Boards

Sailboarding is also known as windsurfing.

"Sailboarders" use a special surfboard that has a mast and sail mounted on it. "Stand-up paddle surfers" use a stable, extra-long board and a paddle. Riders can paddleboard even in calm water. "Skimboarders" use thin, flat boards that are about 3 feet (1 m) long to "skim" over the water.

Skimboards are also called "sleds." Riders slide across a thin layer of water near shore.

Stand-up paddle surfing can be done in lakes and rivers, as well as oceans and seas.

Duke Kahanamoku Statue on Oahu

Surfers find waves throughout the world. Hawaii, where surfing first began, is one of the top spots. Duke Kahanamoku first made surfing popular there in the 1920s. Today's top surfers still take to the great waves found around Oahu, Maui, Kauai, and the Big Island.

SURF

"If you're gonna surf pipeline well, ya gotta just charge it." ~Kelly Slater

Surf City

California was the prime spot for surfers in the 1960s, and that continues today. There are many Southern California surf areas, but Huntington Beach in Orange County is home to several surfing championships. It is often known as "Surf City."

Xtreme Quote

"It's a different wave when it's bigger... I am sure a lot of the guys haven't surfed Huntington like that."
~Brett Simpson, 2009 US Open Winner

Australia

South Africa

Costa Rica

Indonesia

DANGERS

While sharks, jellyfish, and other marine life pose risks to people in the water, the greatest danger to surfers is getting struck by their own surfboards, or being "dropped-in on," colliding with another surfer.

AND RISKS

"It's death on a stick out there."
~Anonymous Surfers

WARNING
DANGEROUS
MARINE LIFE
HAS BEEN
SPOTTED IN
THIS AREA

29

Aerial Tricks
When a surfer and board launch into the air to perform special movements above the water.

Crest
The top of a wave.

Dropped-In On
When a second surfer catches a wave in front of another surfer who is already riding that same wave. This is considered wave "theft" by surfers, and is found to be both rude and dangerous.

Duke Kahanamoku
A Hawaiian surfer often referred to as "the father of modern surfing." Born in Honolulu in 1890, his surfing skills re-popularized the sport in Hawaii and around the world in the 1900s. He was also an Olympic gold medal swimmer.

GLOSSARY

Gun
Short for "big-wave gun." A longer, more streamlined surfboard designed for riding the biggest waves.

Hardwood Board
Surfboards made out of such woods as redwood, balsa, mahogany, or pine.

Maneuverable
Able to move easily.

Polynesia
A group of about 300 islands in the Pacific Ocean, including Hawaii, the Marquesas Islands, Samoa, the Cook Islands, and French Polynesia.

Trough
The lowest part of a wave, or the low point between two waves.

INDEX